TALES OF THE TIME DRAGON

❄RACING❄ THE WAVES

BY ROBERT NEUBECKER

SCHOLASTIC INC.

You are about to travel back in time to New York City in the year 1851.

You'll go south on a trip to the bottom of the world, then head north to California.

For the Weilenmann School of Discovery.

Library of Congress Cataloging-In-Publication Data
Neubecker, Robert, author.
Racing the waves / by Robert Neubecker.
p. cm. – (Tales of the time dragon ; 2)
Summary: On their second adventure, Red the Time Dragon transports Joe and Lilly to the Flying Cloud, a clipper ship on a record-setting trip from New York to San Francisco in 1851.
ISBN 978-0-545-54903-5 (hardcover) – ISBN 978-0-545-54904-2 (paperback.)
1. Flying Cloud (Clipper-ship)-Juvenile fiction. 2. Dragons-Juvenile fiction. 3. Time travel-Juvenile fiction. 4. Sailing ships-Juvenile fiction. [1. Flying Cloud (Clipper-ship)-Fiction. 2. Dragons-Fiction. 3. Time travel-Fiction. 4. Clipper ships-Fiction.] I. Title.
PZ7.N4394Rac 2014
 [E]-dc23

                    2014000788

12 11 10 9 8 7 6 5 4 3 2 1   14 15 16 17 18 19/0

Printed in the U.S.A.   40
First printing, September 2014

Lilly spotted something new in Mr. Miller's class.

"What is it?" asked Joe.

"A ship in a bottle," said Lilly.

"I know that! What kind of ship?"

Lilly looked closer. "A clipper ship."

To the library!
Lilly sat down at the computer and began to type.

C-L-I-P-P-E-R

S-H-I-P

"Red!" Lilly cried as she and Joe spotted their friend the Time Dragon.

"Call me First Mate Red! Come aboard our clipper ship, the *Flying Cloud*!" Red said proudly. "It's June of 1851, and the California gold rush is on. Our clipper ship is fast, one of the fastest ever. . . .

"We are sailing from New York, way down around the tip of South America, then up to San Francisco!"

"Why go by ship?" Lilly asked.

"Wagon trains are risky and dangerous. It's faster and safer by sea — most of the time. . . . "

"We sail with Captain Perkins Creesy. Our ship carries everything you need to dig for gold in California: candles, shovels, boots, and more."

"Ahoy there! Welcome aboard!" said the captain.

The *Flying Cloud* filled her sails with wind. The voyage had begun!

The ship headed south.

Red said, "It's warm now, but soon it will get colder. June is summer in New York, but winter in South America. We sail from summer to winter, and then back to summer!"

Red steered the ship because he was very strong.
It often took two sailors to handle the wheel in a
storm.

To guide the ship you had to know your math. The ship's navigator was the captain's wife, Eleanor Creesy. And Ellen was very, very good at math.

She used the sun and stars to find their exact spot on the ocean.

"When the sky is cloudy, I can take our speed, direction, and last known position to plot our course," she told Joe and Lilly. "We are going to sail as fast as we can."

"Ellen is the most important person on the ship," Captain Creesy said. "But don't tell the crew that."

Off the coast of Brazil, whales swam close to the ship and blew huge spouts of water into the air.

The sailors caught lots of fish. "Hurrah!" they cheered.

"Yuck!" said Lilly.

Joe shivered. "It's getting colder," he said.
Ellen brought warm coats from the cabin.
"We're sailing closer to the south pole," she
explained. "Soon we will round Cape Horn, the very
tip of South America. We will have to be careful.
The waters there are the stormiest in the world."

Ellen guided the ship between the islands and the icebergs at the bottom of the world.

The wind grew stronger. The waves got bigger. The air got colder and colder.

The *Flying Cloud* raced up huge waves and plunged down the other side.

Lilly and Joe hung on to Red.

Captain Creesy had the crew take down most of the sails so they wouldn't be torn to pieces.

"Isn't climbing up there dangerous?" asked Joe.

"Very," said Red. "If a sailor falls, he'll die. But if the crew doesn't lower the sails, we all might."

The wind and waves swept the ship backward.
It took all of Red's strength to hold the wheel
steady.

"If we hit the rocks, the ship will go down!"
Ellen cried.

Even worse, it started to snow. Soon the snow became a blizzard.

"Turn the ship around!" Ellen told the captain.

"I wish we could help," said Joe.

Lilly looked around. "I think the best way to help is to stay out of the way. . . . "

At last the storm died down and a lucky wind started to blow. Ellen charted a new course and headed the ship back to Cape Horn.

The *Flying Cloud* rounded the Horn in fine, clear weather.

"Look at all the birds!" Joe cried.

"They sure fly fast," said Lilly.

Red grinned. "Not as fast as the *Flying Cloud*."

"Now we turn north toward San Francisco," Red said as he spun the wheel.

They were headed back toward the equator and back to summer. The wind picked up, strong and steady.

As the ship raced along, Ellen dropped a knotted rope into the ocean. She counted the knots as they ran out.

"More knots mean more speed," she said.

Joe counted and scratched his head. "Eighteen knots?"

Red winked. "That's over twenty miles per hour! I think this trip could break the world record for speed!"

But then the wind stopped.

"We are in the Doldrums," Red explained.

"It's a part of the ocean that has very little wind," sighed Ellen. "Sailors can get stuck here for weeks, even months."

"Not now!" said Captain Creesy. "We're so close to breaking the record!"

Red thought for a minute. "Isn't there an old legend that says a sailor can whistle up the wind?"

"I can whistle!" said Joe.

"Me too!" Lilly piped up.

"We can all whistle!" said the sailors.

Captain Creesy barked, "Well then, on my order,

ALL TOGETHER

WHISTLE!"

Red whistled loudest of all.
Well, actually, he

BLEW!

Eighty-nine days after the *Flying Cloud* set sail
from New York, she dropped anchor in San Francisco
Bay.

It was the fastest time ever!

Lilly hugged Ellen. "You did it!"
"We all did!" said Red.
Captain Creesy smiled. "And we'll do it
again, even faster next time."

"Wait a minute!" Joe squeaked. "It's been eighty-nine days since we left?"

"Mr. Miller's going to be really mad," groaned Lilly.

"Don't worry!" said Red. "With a little computer magic, I can have you back by lunch. See you again soon!"

"Bye, Red!" said the kids.

"I'm starving," said Joe. "What's for lunch?"

Lilly giggled. "FISH."

More About Clipper Ships

Clipper ships were very fast sailing boats that were popular in the middle of the 1800s. They had three masts and large sails. They carried passengers and valuable cargo.

The *Flying Cloud*

Perkins and Eleanor Creesy were real people. They sailed the *Flying Cloud* all over the world. Their world record for sailing speed stood for 136 years. The members of Captain Creesy's crew were a colorful bunch, from all over the world.

People have always worked hard to be the fastest, strongest, and first to succeed.

1851, The *Flying Cloud* sails on its record-breaking trip

1891, Reporter Nellie Bly travels around the world faster than anyone before

Navigation

During the day, Ellen Creesy used a tool called a sextant to navigate. When she looked at the sun through the sextant, she could measure how high it was in the sky. She used this information to help her find their exact spot on the ocean. At night, she used the position of the stars.

The Gold Rush

Clipper ships sometimes carried cargo to California. In 1849, gold was discovered there. Men called "forty-niners" rushed west to get rich. A few did, but life was very hard. Many became farmers and shopkeepers.

1912, The *Titanic* becomes the largest ship to sail the seas

TODAY

1969, Astronauts first land on the moon

Glossary

Bay – An indent in the shoreline where ships are safe from wind and waves.

Blizzard – A big snowstorm.

Doldrums – The part of the ocean near the equator that has very little wind.

Equator – An imaginary line around the center of the earth that divides the northern half from the southern half.

Knot – A measure of speed used at sea that equals 1.15 miles per hour.

Mast – A tall pole that supports the sails of a ship.

Navigator – The person who guides a ship on its voyage.

Voyage – A long trip.